Edward Austin Sheldon

First Reading Book

in easy and familiar words. Designed to accompany the phonic reading

cards

Edward Austin Sheldon

First Reading Book
in easy and familiar words. Designed to accompany the phonic reading cards

ISBN/EAN: 9783337390303

Printed in Europe, USA, Canada, Australia, Japan

Cover: Foto ©Andreas Hilbeck / pixelio.de

More available books at **www.hansebooks.com**

PREFACE.

This little book is designed to accompany the Phonic Reading Cards. For fuller directions as to method of teaching these, see "Elementary Instruction."

Although these lessons are arranged with reference to the method of teaching reading there laid down, they may be very advantageously used independently of them, as an introduction to any ordinary reading book.

By the plan here presented, we believe children will learn to read with far more ease and rapidity than by the ordinary methods. The words at the heads of the lessons are first to be learned as such, when the children will be able, for the most part, to prepare their lesson without the aid of the teacher. The class should first read the lesson from the Cards, and then from the books.

The matter of these lessons is arranged and revised from a series published in London, by the "Society for the Promotion of Christian Knowledge."

I.

THE DOG AND THE RAT.

Is. To. Too. Of. Go. He. For.

The dog ran to get a rat.

1*

The rat bit the lip of the dog.

Now the rat has run to the box.

Now he is in the box.

Let the dog go in for him.

The dog is too big to go in.

Let the cat go in to get him.

II.

THE DOG AND THE COW.

O. Do. So. By. May. Say. You. Has.
Was.

The boy has a rod.

The dog is by him.

O boy do not hit the dog.

The dog bit the leg of the red cow.

He was a bad dog to do so.

You may say so to him. But do not hit him.

W. ROBERTS. SC.

III.

THE PUP.

Ned has got a bun.
Let the pup beg for
bit of the bun.

Go off dog.

Let the pup sit by me.

Now the pup is fed.

He may lap in the pan.

Now let him run to the dog.

V.

THE CAT.

Saw. I. Has.

sun is hot to-day.

It is now mid-

Let us sit on the mat.

Tom may sit by us.

The cat can sit in my lap.

O cat do not run off. I can not let you run to the hen.

The hen has an egg in the box. I saw it in the box.

VI.

THE TOM-TIT.

Fy. Are.

A tom-tit is on the log.

He is in the sun.

How gay and fat he is.

Do not go off tom-tit.

O now the cat has got him. She has run up the tree.

I am so sad for the tom-tit.

O fy cat. You are a bad cat to do so.

ROBERTS. SC

VII.

THE TOP AND THE BEE.

As. Why. Eye.

I can see my top. A
bee is on it. Can my top
see me?

2*

No the top can not see you. But the bee can see you.

Why can not my top see me? For it can hum as a bee can hum.

The top has no eye. For it is but a toy. The bee has an eye. Can you not see its eye?

VIII.

OLD ANN LEE.

Old Ann Lee at the cot
is ill. She can not go out
nor get up.—Her boy Tom
has run to us to say so.

May she eat my bun?

No. She is too ill to eat a bun.—But she may eat sop. And she may sip a cup of tea.

We can go to see her by and by.

ROBERTS. SC.

IX.

THE FOX.

Hark. Bark. Form. Sly. Yard.
Fast. Or. Fern. Barn. New.
Nor. What. When.

Do you see the new dog?

It is not a dog. It is a fox.

But hark. He can bark as a dog.

Yes.   But he has not the form of a dog.

May I go to him and pat him?

No.   He will hurt you if you do. He is so sly.   He bit Tom in the hand just now.

How did Tom get him?

The man at the mill got him in a trap.   And he let Tom have him.

But what will Tom do with him? Will he stay in the yard?

Yes.   Tom will tie him up.   And he will lie on the dry fern in that tub.

Will he run off if he is set free?

Yes.   And he can run fast.   He will get off to the dell if he can. Or he may go to the barn.

Then he may get the old hen and eat her up.　For she sits in the barn.

Will the fox eat hens?

Yes.　He will eat the hen and the cock too if he can get him.—It was he that got the cock and hen of the man at the mill.—And so the man set a trap for him.

O bad fox.　I am glad that the man got you in the trap.　I will not play with you nor go to you.

ROBERTS. Sc.

X.

DICK BELL AND THE NEST.

Far. Try. Son. Fly. Know. Bird. Last.

Do you know Dick Bell?

Is he the son of the man at the mill?

Yes. It is he.

I know him. I saw him at play with Ned when I was last at the mill. What can you tell me of him?

He is a bad boy. He will not do as he is bid. I saw him go up a tree for the nest of a bird. The tree is the big elm by the pond. The nest is not far from the top of the tree. It is the nest of a black-bird. You can see it in the tree. You can just now see the old bird fly out from the nest. John the milkman told him not to go up. I told him so too. And I told him how sad a bird is when her nest is lost. But he went. He got far up into the tree. But he did not get what he went for.

Did he try to get the nest?

Yes. He did try to get it.

But tell me how it was that he did not get it. Did he not go so far up the tree?

Yes. He went up the tree as far as the nest, and he held out his hand to get it.—When he held out his hand to get the nest he let go of the tree. And so he fell in to the pond. I was on the bank and saw him drop.

XI.

DICK BELL IN THE POND.

Such.	One.	Low.	Drew.	Path.
Much.	Into.	Hard.	Girl.	Farm.
	Warm.	Dirt.	Wish	

How did Dick Bell get out of the pond? Can he swim?

No. Dick can not swim. But the pond was low. So that he had not to swim. He got to the bank. But then he fell back and sank in the mud. I will tell you how he got out at last. A man was in the farm yard not far off. And I ran and told the man to help me.—He was a kind man and went to get a long rod out of the barn. We then held out the rod to Dick. He held on to the rod and so we drew him up the bank. He had one bad slip. But the man held him by the hand. And at last we got him up on the path.

Was he much hurt?

No. But he was wet. And

he was in a sad mess with the mud.

How did he get dry?

. He went into a cot that was hard by. And we got a kind girl to dry him and warm him and rub off the dirt. But he is now ill from the wet. And I do not know when he will get well.

You must not play with Dick Bell. He was a bad boy not to do as he was bid. And he was a bad boy to try to get the nest of the black-bird. I am glad that he did not get it. And I hope that he may not try to do such a bad act when he gets well. If so, I shall not be sad that he fell in to the pond.

ROBERTS. SC.

XII.

THE AXE.

Your.   Sharp.   Chop.   Thing.   Stool.
Stir.   Foot.

I have a bad toe.   Can you tie a bit of rag on it?

Yes.   I have a bit of rag.   Let

me see your toe. Did you cut it?

No. But Dick Bell cut it.

How did Dick Bell cut your toe? Was he at play with you?

Yes. He was at play with me. And he cut my toe with an axe.

Did I not tell you not to play with Dick Bell? You know that he is a bad boy.—You saw him try to take the nest of the black-bird, when he fell into the pond.—But tell me what Dick was at with the axe. And how did he get it?

He was at play with me in the copse. A man had left his axe on a log.—Dick got the axe to try to chop the log with it. But he let it slip out of his hand on to my big toe.

Did you not tell him that it is bad to play with an axe?

Yes. I told him so. And I told him not to get the axe, lest he hurt my hands or his own.

Well. Now you see what a bad thing it is to play with an axe. Dick did not cut your hands nor his own. But he has cut your toe. And that was as bad. It is well he did not cut your toe off

Is it a bad cut?

No. It is not a bad cut. I will tie this rag on it. The dirt must be kept from it. And you must lay your toe up. You must not run nor stir. You must sit still and set the foot up on a stool. It will then be well in a day or so.

XIII.

HOW TO GET WARM.

Air.

Do not sit by the fire.

But I am so cold. I do not know what else to do.

I will tell you then what else you can do.—Go out in to the air, and run, and jump, and skip, and hop. Or you may play with the dog. And then you will get warm.

But I can not go from the fire.

It is so warm by the fire, and so
cold out in the yard.

But you know that you must go
out by and by. And then you will
be cold.—You can not 'help that.
But run and jump, and get warm
now. And you will not be cold

then.—You will be ill if you stay too much by the fire.

Well, then, I will go out and skip and play with Tray.—Now, Tray, let us go to the yard. Jump up on this bench.—You can jump as well as I can. Now jump down.—Try to run as fast as I can. Do not bark.—But let us see if we can get the bird that sits on that tub. No. He is off.—And I can tell you that he is glad to get off. See how far he is now up in the air.—You can not run as fast as the bird can fly. And I find that I can not run as fast as you can.—Now, Tray, you and I are warm. We will go in.

Well, are you warm yet?

O, yes. I am so warm. I am glad that I did not stay by the fire. I shall not now go to the fire when I am cold. But I shall go out, and run and play in the air.

XIV.

THE HAY RICK.

Put. Were. They. First. House. Fork. Does. Grass. Girls.

What is hay?

Hay is dry grass. Did you not see men and boys and girls toss the hay up, and turn it when the days were long and warm?

O, yes. I saw them toss the hay

ROBERTS. Sc

up with long forks.   But how do
they first get the hay?

It is first grass.   When the grass
is grown up, they cut it.—Then they
let it lie in the sun.   And so it lies
till what is at the top is dry.—Then
they toss it and turn it with a fork

4

as you saw.—And when it is dry they put it in to a rick. So that cows may eat it when the days are cold as they are now, and the grass will not grow.

The rick is in the form of a house. And straw is on the top.—Tell me why they put the hay in to the form of a house?

The wet runs off the top of the rick just as it runs off the top of a house.

But will the wet hurt the hay?

Yes. The hay rots if it gets wet. And if at first it does not lie in the field till it is dry, it gets first warm, then hot, and at last it burns.—I saw a hay rick burnt in this way at the farm on the hill.

I can use a fork. I shall be glad when the days are warm and long, that I may go out and toss and turn the hay.

XV.

THE FROG.

Where. There. Fish. Watch.

Where did you go just now? I saw you go out.

I went to the pond to see the fish swim.

What have you got in your hand?

It is a frog. I got him in the long grass by the pond. Do you see him try to get out of my hand?

Yes. I see him try. But let him go. You hurt him.

No. I do not hurt him. I do but hold him fast.

But you do hurt him. That is why you see him try so hard to get free.—It is to him as if a great man were to hold you fast in his hand.

Is it so? I did not think of that. I will let him go then.

There now. See how fast he hops off. He can not thank you. But you can see how glad he is.

O yes. And I am glad to see that he is glad. But I did not think that I hurt him.

I know that you did not think so. You did not think at all.—You know that frogs and birds and dogs and cats can not tell you when you hurt them.—So you must think of what you do to them. And you must watch them. You may then see when you hurt them.

4*

XVI.

THE FROG IN THE POND.

Swan. Does. Arms. Thin.

I saw the frog hop in to the pond.
Let us go and see him swim.

There he is by the tree. You
may stir the pond with your stick

if you will. You will then see how fast he will be off.

O, how well he can swim. But he does not swim as a fish swims.

No. He has not fins as a fish has. He swims with his legs. Just as a man swims with his legs and arms.

Can you swim as he can?

I can swim in the way that he swims. But I can not swim so fast nor so long.—It is not God's will for men to swim as well as frogs do. Men stay on land and go into the sea but now and then.—But watch this frog, and you will see that he stays as long in the pond or in the ditch as he stays on the land.—I will tell you how it is that I can not swim so well as he can.—I have not a web to my toes and hands such as he has.—You can see that he has a web or thin skin from toe to toe. It is like the web on the toes of a duck. The birds that swim have webs of this kind.

Then the swan has webs to his toes?

Yes. You may see that he has when you next go to the pond.

XVII.

TRAY AND FAN.

Could.   Come.   Would.   Care.   Things.

We have two dogs.

What are their names?

Tray and Fan.   Tray is a big dog,
and Fan is a little one.

Which do you like best?

Oh! I like Fan best. I do not like Tray.

Why do you not like Tray?

He is so big. And he jumps up on me when I go near him.

But do you know of what use he is? He is of much more use than Fan.

Of what use is he then?

I will tell you. If bad men should come to steal what is in the house he would bite them.—And if we were in bed he would bark and wake us. And then we could take care of our things.

XVIII.

OLD ANN LEE.

Thank.   Good.   Bye.   Work.

Old Ann Lee is well now.   I saw her to-day.   She is blind.   But she can sit, and knit, and spin.

Shall we go and see her?

Yes.   We will go by the field.

There she is.   She sits by the door of her cot, and spins.

How do you do, Ann Lee ?

I am well, my dear, thank God! I am now blind.   But I can spin, and knit, and go to church.

How do you find your way to church ?

My son Tom leads me there.

Good bye, Ann Lee.   We will take care to come and see you now and then.   And send to us if we can help you.

Thank you.   Good bye, my dears.

Now then we will go home.   Do you know Tom Lee ?

Yes. I see him when he leads old Ann to church.

He is a good son. He is so kind to her.

How old is he?

He is but ten years old.

Does he work at the mill?

Yes. He works hard at the mill. And he takes home all he gets for his work to old Ann.

He is a good boy. And if he keeps on so he will be a good man.

Does Tom Lee like play?

O, yes. He likes play as well as Dick Bell does.

But I do not see him at play.

No. He has no time for play.

5

He works hard all day. And when he goes home he reads to old Ann.

XIX.

THE RAT.

Whose.   Look.   Shell.   Squirrel.   Full.
Two.   Wood.   Teeth.   Marmot.   Gnaws.
Gnaw.   Mouth.

O, here is a rat in the trap.

What an old one he is!

How can you see that he is an old one?

He has such long teeth.

But why has an old rat long teeth?

An old man's teeth are not long.

And our old dog Tray has not long

ROBERTS. Sc.

teeth.   The pup's teeth are as long
as Tray's teeth.

I will tell you why.   A rat's teeth
grow as long as he lives.—But when
you are a man, your teeth will grow
no more.—And a dog's teeth grow
no more when he is of his full size.

Can you tell me why a rat's teeth grow as long as he lives?

Yes. The rat does not bite what he eats as you do. And he does not tear it as you see Tray tear meat from a bone.—He gnaws it into little bits like saw-dust with the two long teeth which you see in the front of his mouth.—And if the teeth were not to grow he would soon wear them out. For he gnaws hard things that lie in his way as well as what he eats.

Can he gnaw wood?

Yes. If you were to stop up his hole with wood to try to keep him in, he would gnaw a hole in the wood.—I once saw a large piece of lead put on the hole of a rat.   But the rat made a hole in the lead and got out.

But why does not this old rat gnaw his way out of the trap with his long teeth?

There is tin in the trap on the sides.   And he can not gnaw tin, for it is too hard.

O, now I see that my squir-rel has two teeth in the front of his mouth like the rat's teeth.   Will they grow as long as he lives?

Yes.   Look at your squir-rel when he eats a nut, and gnaws a hole in the shell.—You will then see how he would wear down his teeth if they were not to grow.

5*

What beasts are there which gnaw what they eat like the rat and the squir-rel, and whose teeth grow as long as they live?

You know one that has the same kind of teeth. Can you not tell me his name?

Is it the cat?

No. There is the cat. Look at her mouth. You will then see that she has not teeth like the rat to gnaw with. · Her ·teeth are more like the dog's.

O, do you mean the rab-bit?

Yes. If you go to him and give him this leaf, and look at him while he eats it, you will see his teeth. And you will see how he makes use of his teeth.—Then there is the hare which eats in the same way. And there is the mar-mot, a strange little thing that lives in a land a great way off.

XX.

HANDS AND PAWS.

Color. Their. Mouse. Dormouse. Large.
Eyes. Young. Thumb. Monkey. Paws.

What have you got in that little box?

Look at it. What do you suppose it is?

It seems like a young squirrel.

But it is not a squirrel, if it does look like one. Is it not like some-

thing not so big as a squirrel, that you have seen?

O, I know what you mean. It is like a mouse.

Yes. This is a mouse. Its name is the Dor-mouse.

Its color is brown. He has a

large tail, too. And his fine black eyes are just like my squirrel's.

Yes. And you will see by and by that he eats like a squirrel.

O, now he sits up on his hind legs. And he holds a nut in his two hands. And he gnaws it just as the squirrel does.

You must not say his hands, but his fore feet.

But he can hold a nut as I hold an apple in my hands.

Yes. But he can not hold a nut in one paw. And you can hold an apple in one hand.

O, I see that he takes hold with both paws But why can he not hold a nut in one paw?

He has not a thumb as you have. And so he can not pinch a thing as you can.—He has four toes in a row on each of his fore feet. And he has five toes on his hind feet, like the toes on your foot.—Look at your foot and your hand. You will then see that your great toe is not put on your foot as your thumb is put on your hand.

Have no beasts thumbs as I have?

Yes. Apes and monkeys have thumbs. And they can pinch a thing with one hand as you can. But a monkey has four hands and no true feet.

O yes. I have seen a monkey

take hold of the branch of a tree by his hind foot.

There are monkeys that can take hold of the branch of a tree by their tails as well as by their hands or feet.

Where did you get this Dor-mouse?

John Bell got it in a hole in a tree. It was a-sleep when he got it.

ROBERTS. Sc.

XXI.

THE DORMOUSE.

Been. Found. Some. All. Comes.
Ground. Done.

Had your dor-mouse been a-sleep for some
weeks when John Bell found him? And
did he not eat at all for that time?

I can not say that it did not eat for all that time. But it did not eat much. Would you like to have me tell you how the dormouse lives ?

O, yes ; do. I like him, and would like to know all you can tell me of him.

I will tell you then how he lives in summer and in win-ter. You know that the days are hot in sum-mer. Then he sleeps a little while in the day and wakes at dusk. He eats and plays as he likes all night. He runs up and down the trees and jumps from branch to branch.—But when win-ter comes near, the days are cold. And then he finds out a snug hole in a tree or in the ground. He makes a nest in the hole. The nest is made of leaves and grass.—He next gets such nuts and seeds as he can. And these he stores up in his hole. When he has done this, he curls up in his nest and goes to sleep.

How long does he sleep?

As long as the days are cold. When a mild day comes, he wakes up and eats a nut or two from his store. When the cold comes back, he goes to sleep as he did at first. And so he goes on till spring comes and the days are warm. Then he comes out of his hole and lives like the rest of the things that live in the woods.

How I wish I had a dor-mouse.

I will give you this one if you will take care of him.

O, thank you. I will take great care of him. I will give him a nice large cage. And I will feed him with the best nuts I can get.

You may take him in your hand if you like.

But will he not bite me as my squir-rel did?

No. He will not bite you if you do not hurt him.

O, how soft he is. I like him so much. He is my pet.

XXII.

THE YAK.

North. Small. Short. Foot.

Snow lies on the ground all the year on the tops of high hills.

Does snow lie on the ground in spots where there are no high hills?

Yes. Far to the North.

Do men live where there is snow all the year?

Yes. Men live there, and boys and girls too.

What do they eat? Can they get bread?

No. They cannot get bread like that which we eat, for they have no wheat. They eat fish and meat.

But how can they get meat?   Are there beasts that live where there is no grass on account of the snow?

Yes.   There are beasts that live on fish. And there is the Deer that lives on moss, which grows when the snow is on the ground. And there is the Yak, a small kind of ox, with short legs, which lives on the tops of high hills.

How does he get his food?

He digs a trench in the snow with his nose, and goes up the hill as he digs. He finds some moss on the ground, which he eats like the deer.—But by and by he gets to a place where the snow is so deep that he cannot work on.

And what does he do then?

He folds up his short legs and rolls down the hill till he comes to the edge of the snow.

But what does he do next?

Then he digs a trench like the first, and so he keeps on till he has had as much moss as he likes.

I would like to see a yak. What an odd beast he must be!

6*

XXIII.

THE BEES.

Honey. Learn. Those. Should. Wasps.

Come with me and look at the bees.'
But do not go too near the hive. If you do
they will sting you.

Why should I look at the bees? I do
not like to look at them so well as at wasps.
They are not so bright and gay as wasps are.

No, they are not so bright and gay. But
they do much more good. And you may
learn more from them if you look at them,
than you can from wasps.

O, I know what good they do. They
make honey and wax. But what can I learn
if I look at them?

Come with me and I will tell you. Do
you not see how hard they work?

I see them move here and there. But I can not see what they do.

But if you look with care you may see what they do. Those that you see fly in to the hive bring loads of honey that they have got from flowers.—Some of the honey they make into wax, to make their combs with, and the rest they stow up in the cells of the comb.

O, now I see some stuff on their legs. What is it?

That is pollen, or dust, out of the flowers. With this they feed their young ones.—Now when you see how hard and how well they work, you should learn to work hard and well like them.—But this is not all you may learn from them.

What else do you mean?

They store up food for the cold time when there will be no flowers for them to go to for fresh honey.—You should in the same way think of the time to come. You should learn to read and write, and to do all the good you can, now you are young.—A time will come when you will have no one to teach you, and no time to learn.

XXIV.

GOD MADE YOU.

Book. Sounds. Think. Arms. Walk.

GOD made you, and gave you all you have.

He gave you eyes to see with, so that you can look at the sun, and the earth, and the beasts that live on it, and the birds that fly in the air. And you can see boys, and girls, and men. And you can read what is in this book.—If you had no eyes you would be blind, and would not see one of these things

by night or by day. When the sun shines,
it would be the same to you as when it is
night.

GOD gave you ears to hear with, so that
ou can hear what we say to you.—And you
an hear sweet sounds when the birds sing
ι the woods and fields, and when GOD's
aise is sung in church.—If you had no

ears you would not hear words nor sweet sounds, but you would be deaf like a stone.

God gave you a mouth to speak with, so that you can talk to boys and girls, and ask for what you would like. And you can say what you think and feel.—If you had no mouth you could not speak, but you would be dumb like a fish.

God gave you arms and hands to work with, and legs to walk, and run, and jump with.—If you had no arms you could do no work. And if you had no legs you would not be able to move, but you must stop in one place like a log.

God gave you a head, so that you can learn what we teach you, and know what it is that you hear and see.

XXV.

GOD SEES YOU.

Dark. Heart. Which. Looks.

GOD is a spirit. He is not like a man. You can not see GOD. But He can see you at all times.—He can see you as well in the night when it is dark, as He can in the day when it is light.—He can see your heart which no man can see. He sees all you do. He hears all you say. He knows all you think, and all you feel.—He is in all places. You can not go out of His sight.

GOD knows when you are a bad boy. He looks on you when you will not do as you are bid. He hears you, if you say what is not true. His eye is on you when you do a bad act.

GOD will not let you be happy when you

will not try to be good.   And it is He who helps you when you wish to be good.

If you pray to God, He will send His Holy Spirit to tell you what you should do, and make you good.

If we mind God, He will make us happy; and when we die, He will raise us up to see Him, and live for ever with the angels.

THE END.

www.ingramcontent.com/pod-product-compliance
Lightning Source LLC
Chambersburg PA
CBHW031242260626
47169CB00007B/2410